Noah's Ark

Noah's Ark

Adapted by Linda Falken

From Genesis, Chapters 6–9

THE METROPOLITAN MUSEUM OF ART

ABRAMS BOOKS FOR YOUNG READERS
NEW YORK

Falken, Linda.

Noah's ark : from Genesis, chapters 6–9 / Linda Falken.

pages cm

Includes bibliographical references and index.

ISBN 978-1-4197-1361-3 (alk. paper)

1. Noah's ark—Juvenile literature. 2. Noah's ark in art—Juvenile literature.

I. Metropolitan Museum of Art (New York, N.Y.) II. Title.

BS658.F35 2014

222'.1109505—dc23

2013044332

Text and art selection by Linda Falken

Book design by Melissa J. Arnst

The text of *Noah's Ark* was adapted from the King James Version of the Bible, Genesis, chapters 6–9.

Published in 2015 by The Metropolitan Museum of Art and Abrams Books for Young Readers, an imprint of ABRAMS. All rights reserved. No portion of this book may be reproduced, stored in a retrieval system, or transmitted in any form or by any means, mechanical, electronic, photocopying, recording, or otherwise, without written permission from the publisher.

Printed and bound in China

10 9 8 7 6 5 4 3 2 1

ABRAMS
THE ART OF BOOKS SINCE 1949

115 West 18th Street
New York, NY 10011
www.abramsbooks.com

THE METROPOLITAN MUSEUM OF ART

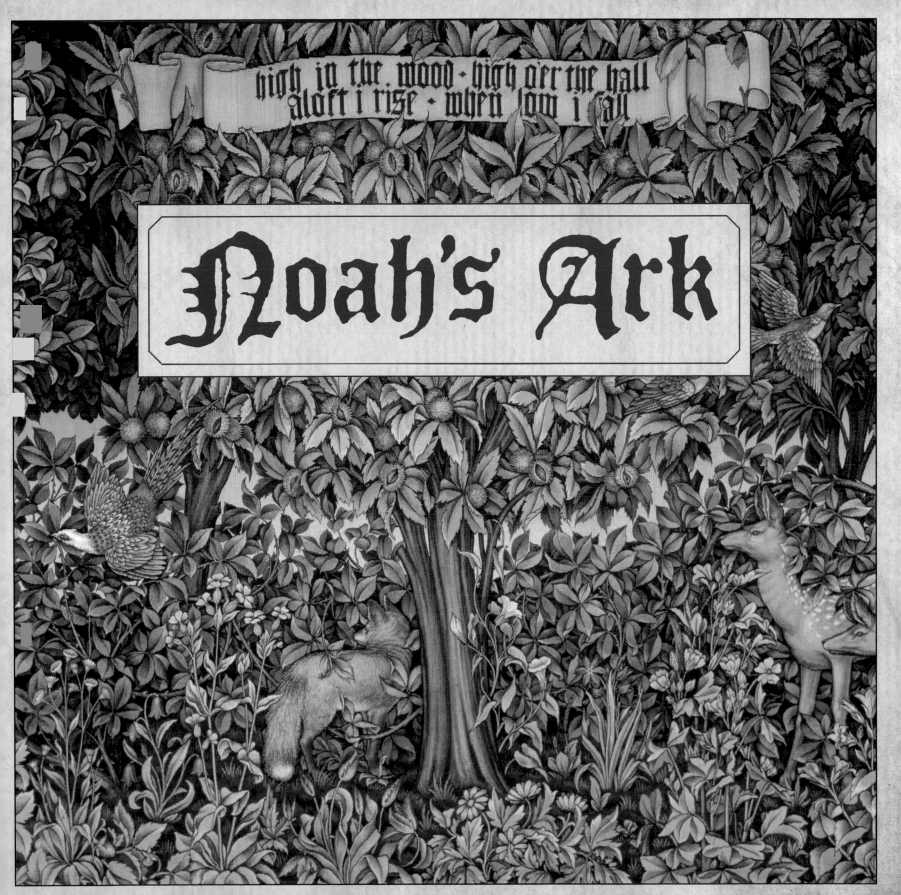

high in the wood · high o'er the hall
aloft i rise · when low i fall

Noah's Ark

Introduction

What is it about the Genesis story of Noah and the flood that has made it resonate in Christian, Jewish, and Islamic cultures throughout the centuries? Why has it inspired countless books and works of art? Why are people today building life-size versions of the ark, while others search for archaeological and geological evidence that the flood actually occurred?

The parable of a great flood that destroys humankind has appeared in many early cultures around the world, from Europe and the Americas to India, China, Australia, and Southwest Asia, from prehistory to the present day.

It's true that myths were used long ago to help explain events that occurred in nature as well as in society. In the tale of Noah, we're told why a rainbow appears in the sky after a storm. But that doesn't explain why the story continues to endure in this age of science and technology, particularly for children.

It may be the story's powerful imagery—from the animals marching two by two onto the ark, to the earth covered in water, the dove returning with an olive branch, and the rainbow of hope—that makes it particularly appealing to children. For adults, these vivid descriptions provide a starting point for discussing the themes of sin and redemption, forgiveness and hope.

Artists, too, have long been fascinated by the imagery in the tale of Noah and the great flood. This book from The Metropolitan Museum of Art features works of art from the fifteenth century to the present day. In a range of media, from tapestries to engravings to paintings, the artists have captured both the fear and the hope inherent in this well-loved parable. And perhaps young artists will be inspired to create their own interpretation of one of the most enduring stories of all time.

It came to pass, when people began to multiply on the face of the earth, God saw that their wickedness was great and their thoughts were evil.

And the Lord said, "I will destroy every thing that I have created from the face of the earth, both humans and beasts, and the creeping things, and the birds of the air, for I am sorry that I have made them."

But among the people, Noah found grace in the eyes of the Lord.

And God said to Noah, "Build an ark of wood, for I will bring a flood of waters upon the earth, and every thing that is in the earth shall die. But you shall go into the ark with your wife, and your sons, and your sons' wives."

And the Lord said, "Of every living thing, two of every sort shall you take into the ark, to keep them alive with you. They shall be male and female. And you shall gather all the food you will need, both for you and for them.

"In seven days, I will cause it to rain upon the earth for forty days and forty nights, and every living thing that I have made will I destroy from the face of the earth."

And Noah did all that the Lord commanded him.

oah gathered the beasts, and the birds, and every thing that crept upon the earth, and took them into the ark, two by two, male and female, as God had said. Then Noah led his wife, and their sons, and their sons' wives into the ark.

And the Lord shut them in.

And after seven days, God made the rain fall upon the earth.

The waters rose and lifted up the ark. And the high hills that were under the whole heaven were covered. The waters rose higher until the mountains were covered, too, and all the earth was flooded as if by one sea.

And the only ones who lived were Noah and his family, and the beasts, and the creeping things, and the birds that were on the ark.

At the end of forty days and forty nights, God made the rains stop.

And Noah opened a window of the ark and sent forth a dove, to see if the waters were gone from the face of the earth. But the dove found no place to rest, and she returned to the ark.

And Noah waited another seven days, and again he sent forth the dove out of the ark. And the dove came back to him in the evening and, lo, in her mouth was an olive leaf. So Noah knew that the waters were receding from the earth.

Noah waited yet another seven days and sent forth the dove, but this time she did not return. And Noah removed the covering of the ark, and saw that the face of the earth was dry.

And God spoke to Noah, saying, "Go forth from the ark, you and your wife, and your sons, and your sons' wives. Bring forth every living thing that is with you, the birds, and the beasts, and every thing that creeps upon the earth, that they may breed and be fruitful, and multiply upon the earth."

And Noah went forth, and his wife, and their sons, and their sons' wives with him. Every beast, every creeping thing, and every bird, male and female, went forth out of the ark.

To honor God for keeping him, and his family, and all the creatures on the ark safe, Noah built an altar and made burnt offerings to the Lord.

And the Lord said, "I will not again curse the ground. Neither will I again destroy every living thing, as I have done. While the earth remains, seedtime and harvest, cold and heat, summer and winter, and day and night shall not cease."

And God said to Noah, "As a sign of my promise to you, after every storm has passed, I shall place a rainbow among the clouds."

Then God blessed Noah and his sons, and said unto them, "Be fruitful, and multiply, and replenish the earth."

Credits

Cover
Noah's Ark, 1857–1907
Currier & Ives, American, 1837–1907
Hand-colored lithograph, 8½ x 12⅜ in. (21.6 x 31.4 cm)
THE METROPOLITAN MUSEUM OF ART, New York
Bequest of Adele S. Colgate, 1962 63.550.434

Nathaniel Currier founded his printing company in 1835. When James Ives became a partner in 1857, the firm took the name Currier & Ives. Between 1835 and 1907, the company created more than four thousand lithographs, including at least four versions of *Noah's Ark*. After the black-and-white pictures were printed, they were usually hand-painted by a group of young women.

Border
Bible and Book of Common Prayer, c. 1607
Robert Barker, British, 1570–1645
Satin worked with silk and metal thread, 13½ x 9¼ in. (34.3 x 23.5 cm)
THE METROPOLITAN MUSEUM OF ART, New York
Gift of Urwin Untermyer, 1964 64.101.1291

The border that frames the text of *Noah's Ark* is from the embroidered cover of a Bible and Book of Common Prayer printed in 1607 by Robert Barker (1570–1645). At the time, Barker held the office of King's Printer, which allowed him to print Bibles and prayer books as well as official documents. Among the Bibles Barker produced was the first edition of the Authorized Version or King James Bible, in 1611.

Pages 2–3, 5
Greenery (detail), 1915
John Henry Dearle, English, 1860–1932, designer; John Martin, tapestry weaving workshop at Merton Abbey, weaver; Morris and Company, manufacturer
Wool and silk, 83½ x 185 in. (212.1 x 470 cm)
THE METROPOLITAN MUSEUM OF ART, New York
Edward C. Moore Jr. Gift, 1923 23.200a

John Henry Dearle was the principal weaver and designer at the Merton Abbey Tapestry Works established in 1881 by William Morris. The founder of the Arts and Crafts movement, Morris hoped to restore the traditions of medieval craftsmanship and revitalize the art and design of industrial England. Dearle created the design for this tapestry in 1892, and it was woven in 1915.

Pages 6–7
Noah Kneeling Before God from *Scenes from Genesis*, 1612
Crispijn de Passe the Elder, Netherlandish, 1564–1637
Engraving, 3⁷⁄₁₆ x 5³⁄₁₆ in. (8.8 x 13.1 cm)
THE METROPOLITAN MUSEUM OF ART, New York
Bequest of Phyllis Massar, 2011 2012.136.714.2

Crispijn de Passe the Elder was an artist and publisher who practiced in four different cities in the Netherlands and Germany, reestablishing his printing business every time he was forced to move because of his Mennonite faith. Together with his children, Crispijn the Younger, Simon, Willem, and Magdalena, de Passe produced thousands of prints during the late 16th and early 17th centuries.

Pages 8–9
God Announcing the Flood to Noah, 17th century
Flemish School
Oil on copper
MUSEO DE ARTE DE QUERÉTARO, Querétaro, Mexico
Photograph: Gianni Dagli Orti / The Art Archive at Art Resource, NY

Unlike Holland, the 17th-century County of Flanders (spread out over present-day Belgium, France, and the Netherlands) remained under the rule of the Spanish Habsburghs, and works of art were primarily religious, as in this painting by an unknown artist. Painting on copper dates back to the mid-16th century. Its smooth, lustrous surface was not only ideal for painting fine detail but also lent a glow to the jewel-like colors of the paint.

Page 11
The Building of the Ark, early 15th century
Miniature from the *Bible Historiale*, the early version (Royal 15 D III, fol. 12)
Workshop of the Boucicaut Master, French, active 1390–1430; Guyart des Moulins, author; Petrus Gilberti, scribe
Colors and gold on parchment
BRITISH LIBRARY, London
Photograph: © British Library Board / Robana / Art Resource, NY

The workshop of the Boucicaut Master was a group of illuminators (artists who decorated manuscripts with paintings and other ornaments) who worked in a similar style, creating works for a variety of clients rather than a single patron. Many of their known works were Books of Hours, but the illumination, or painting, shown here is from an early version of the *Bible Historiale*, a French adaptation of the 13th-century *Historia Scholastica* by Petrus Comestor.

Pages 12–13
The Ark, c. 1700
Lodewijk Tieling, Dutch, active c. 1695–1700
Oil on canvas, 46¼ x 61¼ in. (117.5 x 155.6 cm)
THE METROPOLITAN MUSEUM OF ART, New York
Gift of James DeLancey Verplanck and John Bayard Rodgers Verplanck,
1939 39.184.20

Little is known of Lodewijk Tieling other than that he was a Dutch
landscape artist around the turn of the 18th century. *The Ark* was attributed
to Tieling based on notes from a 1778 auction in Leiden. Tieling's painting
is similar in style and composition to *L'Arche de Noé*, a painting by Cornelis
Snellinck (c. 1605–1669).

Pages 14–15, and details on pages 1 and 32
The Animals Enter Noah's Ark, c. 1555
Aurelio Luini, Italian, c. 1530–1593
Fresco
SAN MAURIZIO AL MONASTERO MAGGIORE, Milan
Photograph: Laurent Lecat / Mondadori Portfolio / Electa / Art Resource, NY

Aurelio Luini belonged to a family of painters in Milan. His father, Bernardino, was
a student of Leonardo da Vinci, and Aurelio, too, was influenced by the great master's
work. His fresco of the animals entering the ark can be seen in one of the chapels of
the Church of San Maurizio in the Monastero Maggiore (Great Monastery) of the
Benedictine order.

Pages 16–17
Marine: The Waterspout, 1870
Gustave Courbet, French, 1819–1877
Oil on canvas, 27⅛ x 39¼ in. (68.9 x 99.7 cm)
THE METROPOLITAN MUSEUM OF ART, New York
H. O. Havemeyer Collection, Gift of Horace Havemeyer, 1929 29.160.35

Gustave Courbet embraced modernity and realism, painting scenes from
everyday life on a large scale previously reserved for scenes drawn from
history. After seeing a waterspout off the Normandy coast, Courbet made
several paintings depicting the phenomenon. In this one, dramatic storm-
tossed seas batter against the rocks as if intent on their destruction.

Page 19
Noah Releases the Dove, 1931
Marc Chagall, French, 1887–1985
Gouache and oil, 25 x 18⁷/₁₀ in. (63.5 x 47.5 cm)
Musée National Marc Chagall, Nice, France
© 2015 Artists Rights Society (ARS), New York / ADAGP, Paris
Photograph: Gérard Blot / © RMN-Grand Palais / Art Resource, NY

Marc Chagall was born in Russia but lived in France for most of his adult
life. It was there that art dealer Ambroise Vollard suggested that Chagall
illustrate the Old Testament of the Bible. In 1931, Chagall created the
gouaches that served as models for the 105 etchings that would take him
until 1956 to complete. The composition of the gouache of Noah releasing
the dove on page 19 is virtually identical to the final etching.

Page 20
The Ark of Noah, 15th century
Miniature from *Le miroir de l'humaine salvation* (Ms. 139. fol. 4r)
Flemish school
Colors and gold on vellum
Musée Condé, Chantilly, France
Photograph: René-Gabriel Ojéda / © RMN-Grand Palais / Art Resource, NY

Le miroir de l'humaine salvation (*The Mirror of Human Salvation*) was a devotional work
first produced in Latin in the early 14th century. Over time, it was translated into several
languages and reproduced in blockbooks (short books produced by woodblock printing)
and illuminated manuscripts. The painting shown here is one of 168 illuminations in a
manuscript that has been in the collection of the Musée Condé since 1841.

Pages 22–23
Noah Leaving the Ark, 16th century
Giulio Bonasone, Italian, active 1531–after 1576
Engraving, 12 x 15¹/₁₆ in. (30.5 x 38.3 cm)
The Metropolitan Museum of Art, New York
Harris Brisbane Dick Fund, 1953 53.600.4223

Born in Bologna, Italy, Giulio Bonasone was a painter and prolific printmaker who worked in
Rome as well as in his native city. In addition to creating his own designs, he made prints based on
works by Michelangelo, Titian, and Parmigianino, among other artists. His engraving of Noah and
his family leaving the ark is modeled after a design by Raphael.

Pages 24–25
Noah's Ark: The Animals Leave the Ark, 17th century
Jacob Bouttats, Flemish, 1660–1718
Oil on panel, 32⁷/₁₀ x 45⁹/₁₀ in. (83.1 x 116.6 cm)
PRIVATE COLLECTION
Photograph: Fine Art Photographic Library, London / Art Resource, NY

Born into a family of artists in Antwerp, Jacob Bouttats learned to paint from his father, Frederik, who was an artist and engraver. Jacob was known for his depictions of the animal kingdom. In this painting, the viewer can almost sense the relief of the animals being released from their long confinement in the ark.

Page 26
Heroic Landscape with Rainbow, 1824
Joseph Anton Koch, German, 1768–1839
Oil on canvas, 42³/₄ x 37³/₄ in. (108.6 x 95.9 cm)
THE METROPOLITAN MUSEUM OF ART, New York
Purchase, Anne Cox Chambers Gift, Gift of Alfred and Katrin Romney, by exchange, and Nineteenth-Century, Modern, and Contemporary Art Funds, 2008 2008.420

Joseph Anton Koch was born in Germany but lived much of his life in Rome. In the early 1800s, the classically trained artist began painting "heroic landscapes," a genre established by French painters Claude Lorrain and Nicolas Poussin in the 17th century. The painting shown here is the fourth and last version of a composition Koch first painted in 1805.